Little Rex
and the BIG ROAR

For my dad, Jim – R.S.
For Alexander and Harry ... Roar! Roar! Roar! – S.J.

First published in Great Britain in 2011
by Piccadilly Press Ltd,
5 Castle Road, London NW1 8PR
www.piccadillypress.co.uk

Designed by Simon Davis
Printed and bound by WKT in China
Colour reproduction by Dot Gradations

ISBN: 978 1 84812 088 4 (paperback)
ISBN: 978 1 84812 089 1 (hardback)

1 3 5 7 9 10 8 6 4 2

A catalogue record of this book is available from the British Library

Little Rex
and the BIG ROAR

Ruth Symes

Illustrated by Sean Julian

Piccadilly Press • London

Rex liked to stomp,
and Rex liked to show his pointiest of pointy teeth
and waggle his sharpest of sharp claws,
but most of all Rex liked to . . .

"Too loud," said Rex's mum.
"Too loud," said Rex's dad.
"Again, again, again!" squeaked Rex's
baby brothers and sister, as they waggled
their baby dinosaur claws
in the air.

Rex tried to roar quietly.
"Roar!"

But it was very hard
not to get louder.
"Roar!"

And then louder still.
"Roar! Roar!
Roar!"

"Too loud," said Rex's mum.
"Too loud," said Rex's dad.
"More, more, more!" squeaked Rex's baby brothers and sister.

"It's time for the babies' nap," said Rex's mum. "No more roaring now, Little Rex." So Rex went to play with his friends.

Rex's friends,
Three-Horns and Spikey,
were playing on the mudslide.
"MAKE WAY FOR REX
THE MUD MONSTER!"
Rex shouted, as he climbed to the top.

From the top of the mudslide Rex could see his mum and dad and his baby brothers and sister.

"LOOK AT ME!" Rex called to them, but Rex's mum and dad and the baby dinosaurs were all snoozing.

Then Rex saw a pterodactyl flying towards
the baby dinosaurs.

He had to do something . . .

Rex slid
down the mudslide,

and ran faster
than he'd
ever run
before
and . . .

just as the
pterodactyl was
about to pounce
on the baby
dinosaurs . . .

The pterodactyl
flew away as fast as
he could.

"Too loud,"
said Rex's mum
and dad, waking up
suddenly.

But then they realised
what had happened.

"YOU SAVED US, REX!"
squeaked the baby dinosaurs,
as they waggled their baby dinosaur
claws in the air.

Rex was a hero.

All the baby dinosaurs wanted to learn
to roar just like Rex . . .